Myths of Legend:
A Bestiary

Written by
Logan Uber

Illustrated by
Megan Withey

Myths of Legend: A Bestiary

© 2017 The Brothers Uber

ISBN: 978-1-943933-84-6

*For Squid and Pickles,
whose boundless love is like a phoenix ever rising.*

History is filled with tales of wondrous creatures. Riddled with stories of dragons and monsters, of unicorns and faithful companions, of things that go bump in the night and scurry in the bright light of day. While not exhaustive in nature, this volume seeks to pull back the curtain and provide a glimpse as to who and what some of those beasts of myth and legend were and are.

Adar Llwch Gwin

A fairy's gift bestowed the beasts
And so it came to be
Imbued with magic
They followed all commands
Always present at the feasts
The castle they would always see
They lived to make life less tragic
And aid to protect their homelands

Bakeneko

With age comes magic
They walk about as humans
The bakeneko

Crocotta
With swiftness it runs
The strength of dog and wolf
With cunning words
It mimics man
A gaze thrice seen
Roots all in their place

Dragon

With moonlit sky
On silent wings
A dragon flies
Her song she sings

Ethiopian Pegasus

Upon the Ethiopian plains
Roam the winged beasts
With two horns upon their heads
And power in their wings
They graze upon the grass
And fly upon the wind

Fire Drake

His claim to fame
A fearsome name
With breath of flame
And focused aim

Griffin

With regal stately grace
And wings like feathered
lace
Crowned with eagle's head
A single mate to ever wed
With nest of treasured gold
All the creatures to be ruled

Hydra
A many headed beast
With serpent's bite
And strength untold
Its breath like poison
Wanderers beware

Imugi

Before a thousand years have passed
And dragons they have become

Lives the benevolent imugi
In caves of water they do hide

Their presence brings good luck
As proto-dragons not yet grown

They live and help and seek to learn
For in a thousand years they grow
To become dragons full of wisdom

Jaculus

With tiny size
And rapid speed
Upon the forest floor
Or flying through the trees
Like lightning with its speed
Its strike is deadly sure
The jaculus is not afraid

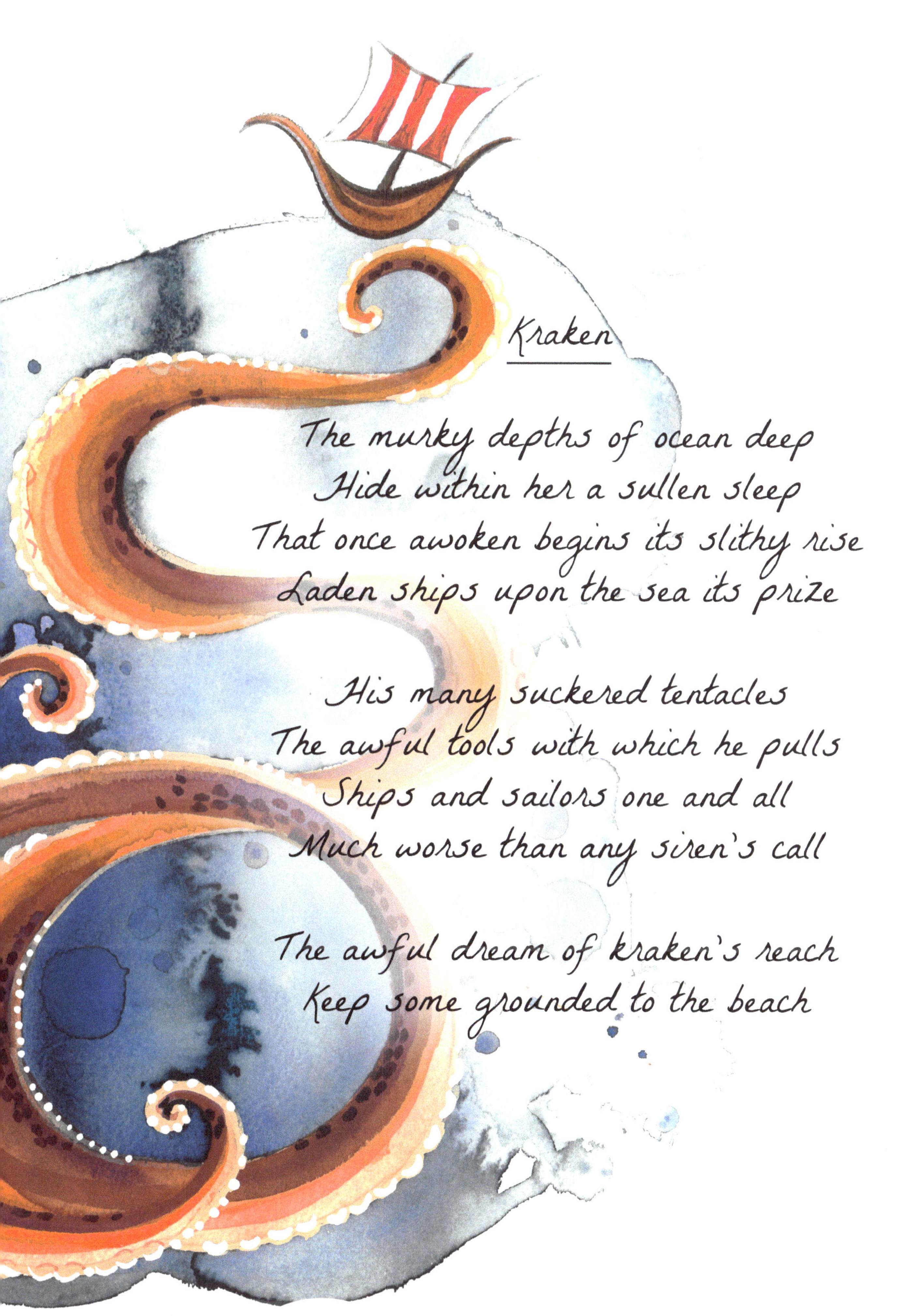

Kraken

The murky depths of ocean deep
Hide within her a sullen sleep
That once awoken begins its slithy rise
Laden ships upon the sea its prize

His many suckered tentacles
The awful tools with which he pulls
Ships and sailors one and all
Much worse than any siren's call

The awful dream of kraken's reach
Keep some grounded to the beach

Lightning Bird

Of clear blue skies
It makes a storm
Casts lightning as it flies
From its winged form

Mngwa

Mystery of the night
Its paw prints found
And stories told
By young and old
Of how it makes no sound
And is ever out of sight

Naga

Her beauty sits upon a serpent's tail
Her gaze causes many men to fail
Within the darkened cave to rest
Her strength unrivaled by the best
With a single poisoned bite
Men lose their will to fight
But seek her guidance patiently
And her wisdom she'll give freely

<u>Oozlum Bird</u>

In myths and legends is found a special bird
With wings that flap and let it fly absurd

At times it flies in circles ever faster
And with each passing loop escapes its
master

And backward through the air they sail
So as to see the feathers of their tails

Phoenix

From ashes rise a flame reborn
With speckled spark of burning red
As if the bonds of death are torn
And fear itself has fled
Each new death becomes the morn
Of birth anew and wings outspread
The bitter grave has lost its thorn
Becoming little more than a simple bed
With no reason to ever mourn
For the phoenix is not long dead

Qilin
_____

When good men pass
And rulers die
When all the people mourn
The qilin comes
And pays respect
It heralds of good times yet to come
An omen of prosperity
And with its coming
Serenity is never far behind

Ramidreju

Once every hundred years or so
A special beast is born
With healing in its fur
And a thirst for gold
Its body long and skinny
With features like a weasel
And a piggish nose to dig deep
holes
It roams throughout the
countryside

Salamander

Born of fire
Life of fire
Harbinger of fire

<u>Tarasque</u>

Once a mighty fearsome beast
With lion's head and six short legs
And body like an ox
On its back a turtle shell
And upon its tail the stinger of a scorpion

It hid upon the river banks within the marshy
land
And perchance a weary traveler would pass its
den
And find their way to a bitter end
For the tarasque would dine upon man and beast
Even boats upon the river felt its wrath

Until beauty passed its way
And with her patience and her charms
She tamed the beast and saved the day

Unicorn

With many fabled tales
Its purity is shared

With perfect beauty
And gentle kindness

A mane of silver
And upon its head
A single horn

Vielfras

Its shaggy fur and cat like claws
Coupled with its doglike shape
And add a bit of hungry fox
And the vielfras you will find

With gluttony its call to life
It spends its days always feasting
And when its full it finds a way
To eat and eat some more

<u>Will o' the Wisp</u>

The wind in the willows that whispers
the way
Wending and winding through the still
of the night
Flitting and floating in glimmering
flight
Marking the way towards a fortuitous
day

Xecotcovach

With fearsome strength
And talons sharp
It flies to fight its foes

With rapid strikes
And claws like steel
It tears and scraps away

Its speed is swift
Its wings like night
Fear it brings to all it fights

Yale

With stately horns and varied gaze
Friend to king and queen
He surveils the mighty kingdom
And defends the realm from foe
And upon the royal coat of arms
His form is often found

Zmaj

With wings and hardened scales
It hunts among the wooded trails
Its roar is loud and grand
Heard throughout all the land
They travel near and far

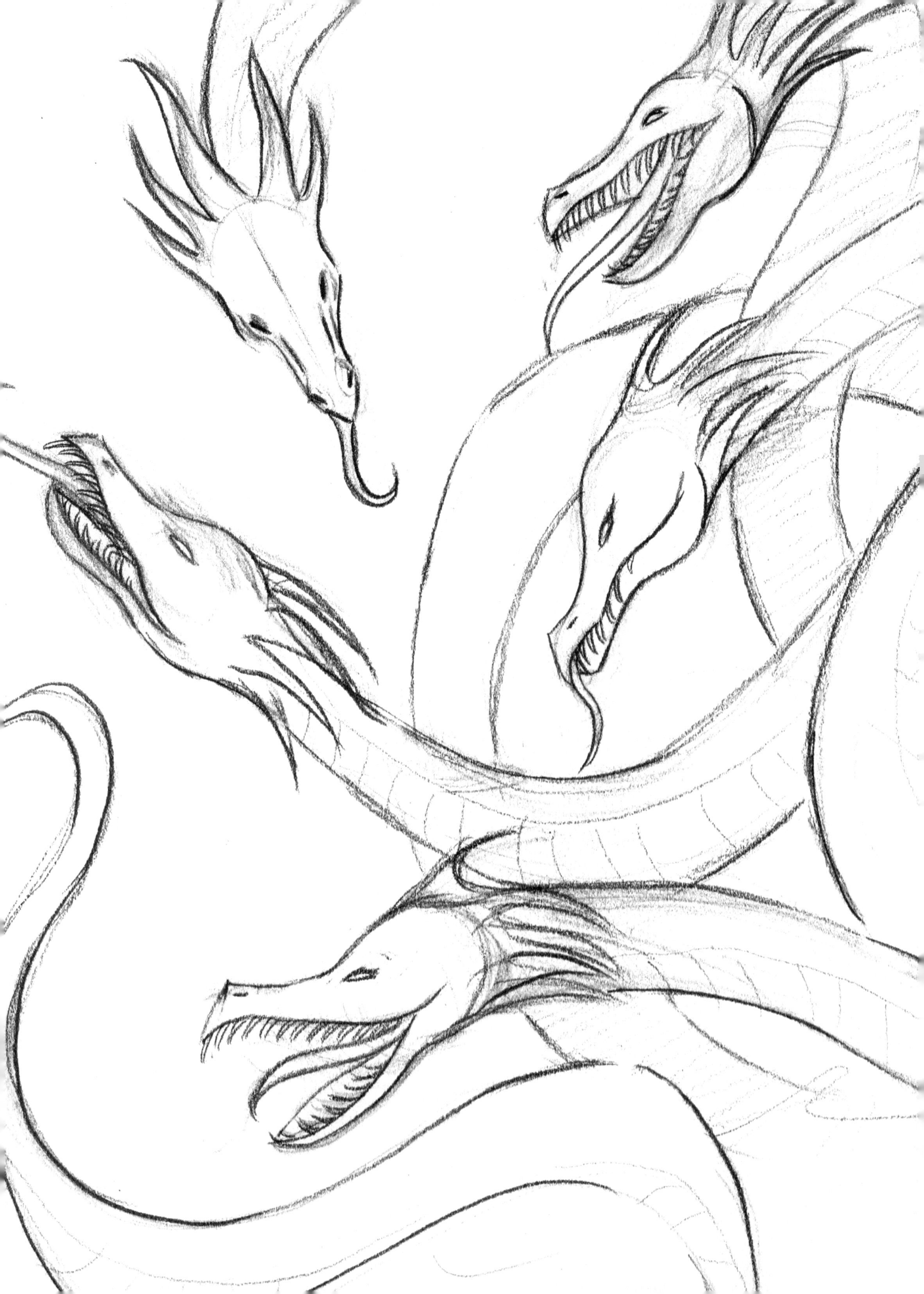

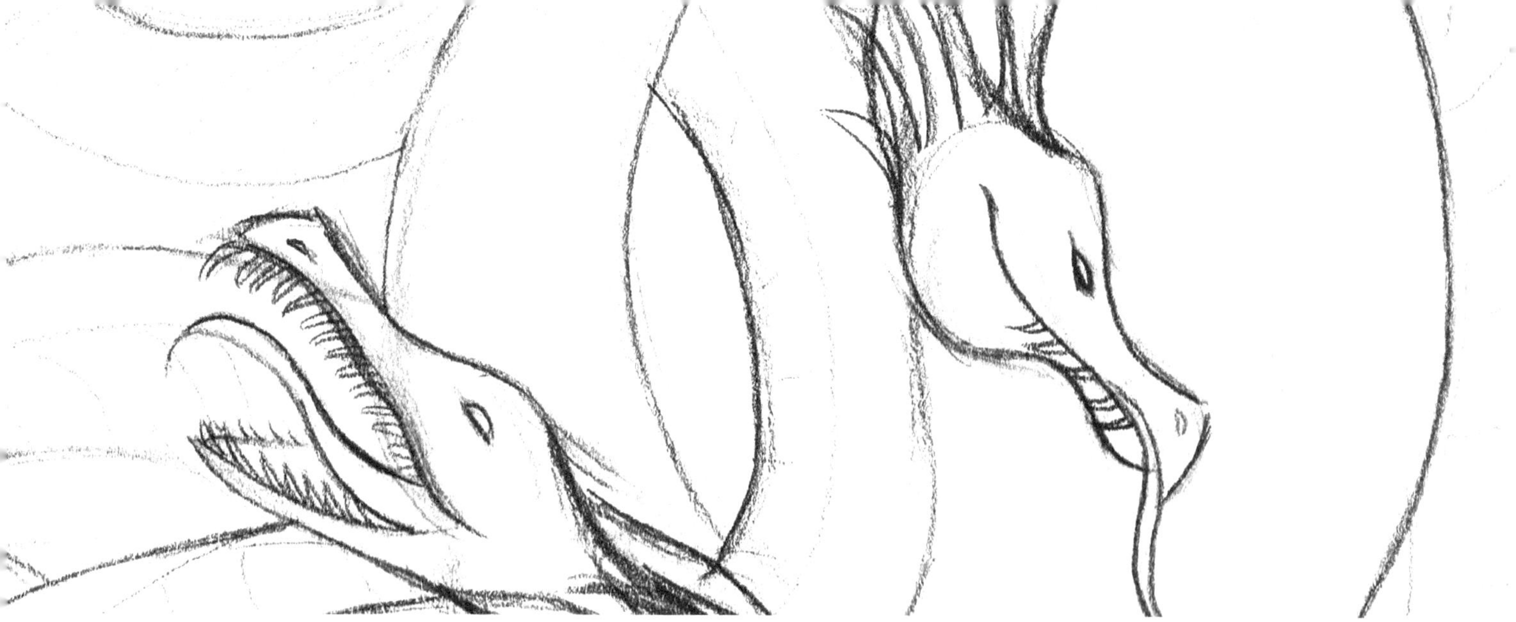

Logan resides in Western Pennsylvania with his small family. He holds a masters of art degree in Intelligence Studies, but his true passions are entrepreneurship, writing, and tabletop game design. He is known for his children's book "Once Upon a Time."

Megan is a Watercolor artist from Wellington, Florida. She attended School of Visual Arts in New York, NY., focusing on abstract painting. She discovered her true passion of children's illustrations as she began making drawings and paintings for her two sons when they were young.

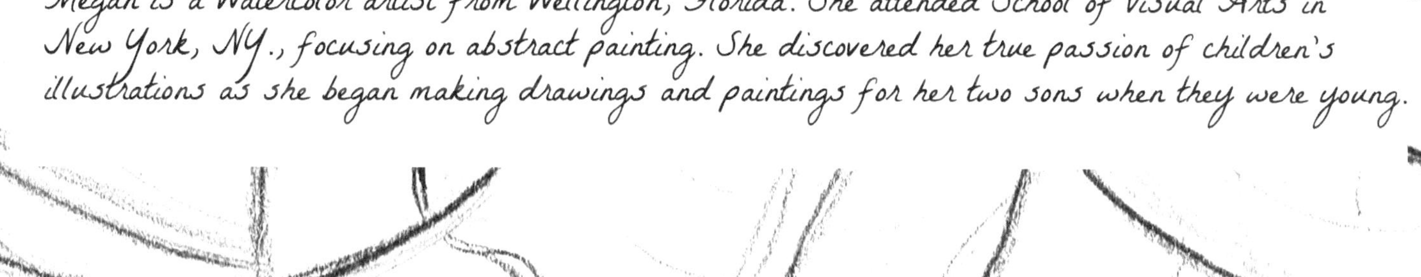

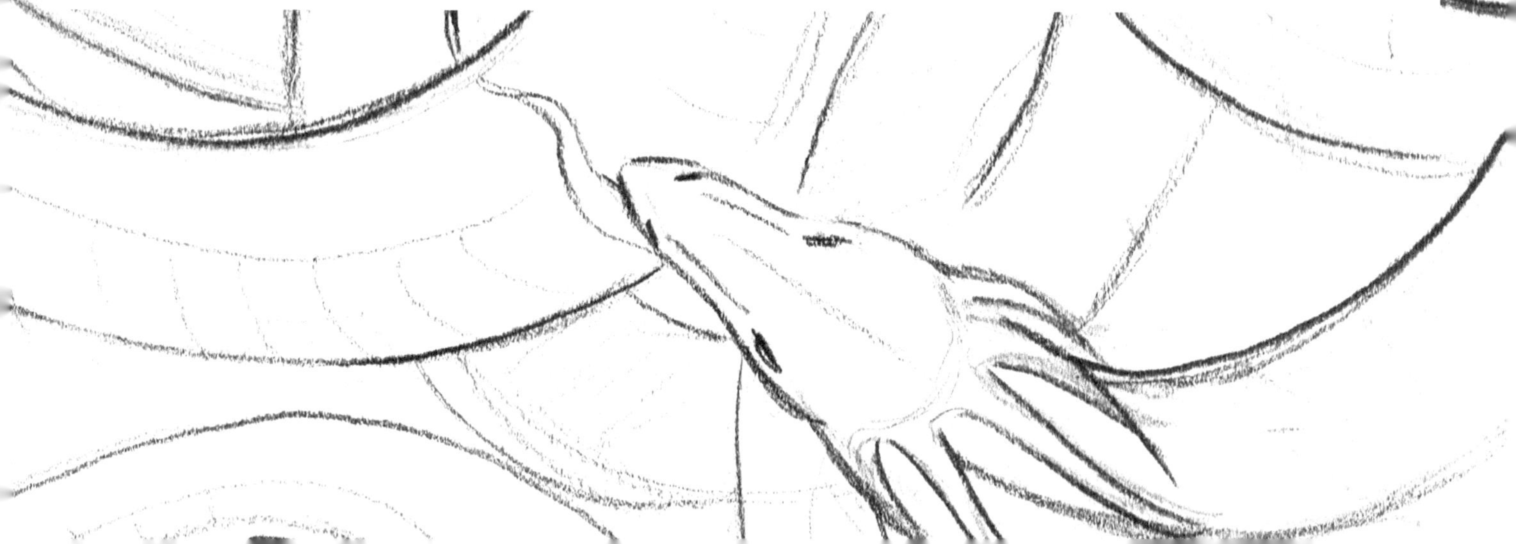